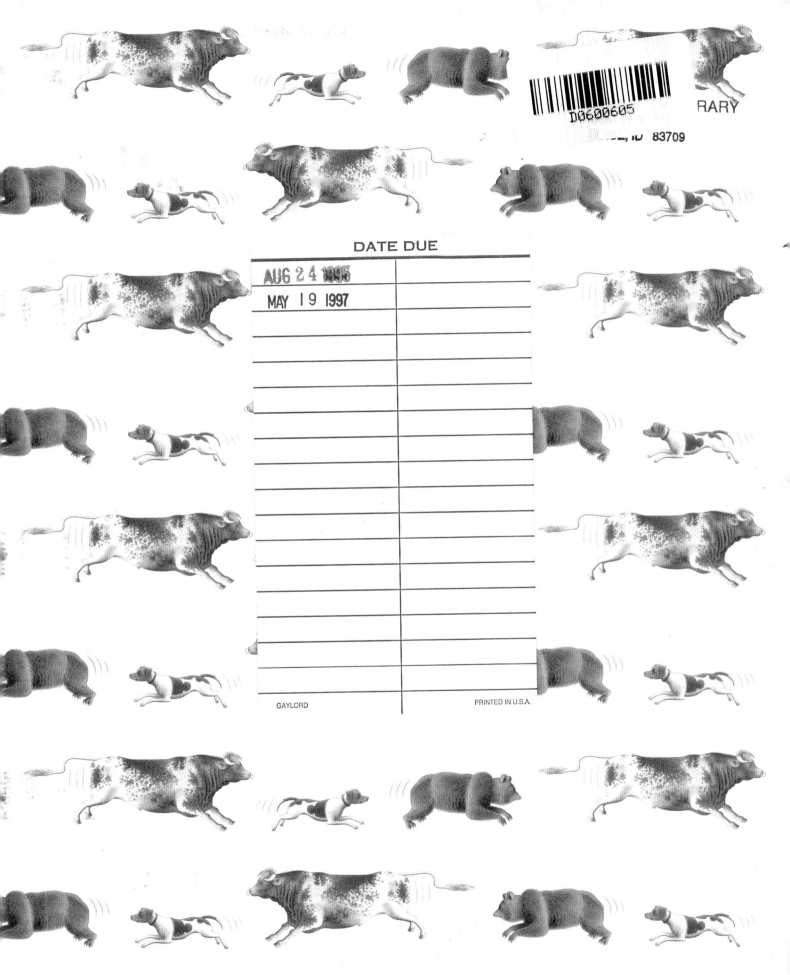

ONCE UPON A TIME...

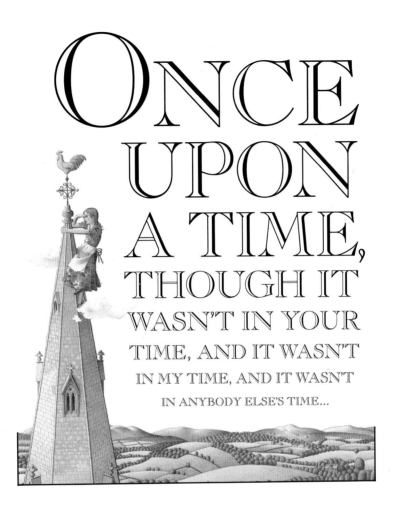

ONCE UPON A TIME,
THOUGH IT
WASN'T IN YOUR
TIME, AND IT WASN'T
IN MY TIME, AND IT WASN'T
IN ANYBODY ELSE'S TIME...

ALAN GARNER

ILLUSTRATED BY
NORMAN MESSENGER

DORLING KINDERSLEY
LONDON • NEW YORK • STUTTGART

A DORLING KINDERSLEY BOOK

First American Edition, 1993
2 4 6 8 10 9 7 5 3 1

Published in the United States by
Dorling Kindersley, Inc., 232 Madison Avenue
New York, New York 10016

Library of Congress Cataloging-in-Publication Data
Garner, Alan, 1934 –
      Once upon a time / retold by Alan Garner : illustrated by Norman
Messenger. – 1st American ed.
          p. cm.
      Contents: The fox, the hare, and the cock – The girl and the
geese – Battibeth.
      ISBN 1-56458-381-3
      1. Tales. [1. Folklore.] I. Messenger, Norman, ill.
II. Title.
PZ8.1.G16820n 1993
398.21–dc20   93-9686
[E]   CIP
                                      AC

Color reproduction by DOT Gradations Ltd.
Printed and bound by Imago, Hong Kong

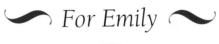 *For Emily*

THE FOX, THE HARE, AND THE COCK

Once upon a time, though it wasn't in your time, and it wasn't in my time, and it wasn't in anybody else's time, but whatever it was, a fox and hare lived by a lake.

When the winter came, the hare made herself a hut of tree bark, but the fox made himself a hut of ice.

"Pooydorda!" said the fox. "Look at you in your tree bark, and me in my glittering ice!"

But in the spring, all the ice melted away, and the fox said to the hare, "Oh, let me in to warm by your fire!"

So the hare let the fox into her hut, but then the fox drove out the hare, and lived in the hut himself.

The hare walked until she met a dog, and the dog said, "What are you crying for?"

"I can't help it," said the hare. "I made a hut of tree bark, and the fox made a hut of ice. He begged me to let him in, and now he drives me out."

"Don't cry," said the dog. "I'll get rid of him."

"No, you won't," said the hare.

"Yes, I shall," said the dog. And he went to the hut, and said:

"Bow-wow-wow! Bow-wow! OUT, Fox!"

But the fox said from the fireside:

> "When I clump, ta-ra!
> When I thump, ta-ra!
> When I jump, ta-ra-ra!
> How the fur flies!"

And at that, the dog was frightened, and he ran away.
And the hare walked on.

She met a bear, and the bear said, "What are you crying for?"

"I can't help it," said the hare. "I made a hut of tree bark, and the fox made a hut of ice. He begged me to let him in, and now he drives me out."

"Don't cry," said the bear. "I'll get rid of him."

"No, you won't," said the hare.
"The dog tried, and he couldn't."

"Yes, I shall," said the bear. And he went to the hut, and said:

"Garrum! Garrum! OUT, Fox!"

But the fox said from the fireside:

"When I clump, ta-ra!

When I thump, ta-ra!

When I jump, ta-ra-ra!

How the fur flies!"

And at that, the bear was frightened, and he ran away.
And the hare walked on.

She met a bull, and the bull said, "What are you crying for?"

"I can't help it," said the hare. "I made a hut of tree bark, and the fox made a hut of ice. He begged me to let him in, and now he drives me out."

"Don't cry," said the bull. "I'll get rid of him."

"No, you won't," said the hare.
"The dog tried . . .

and the bear tried . . .

and they couldn't.

"Yes, I shall," said the bull. And he went to the hut, and said:

"Harroo! Harroo! OUT, Fox!"

But the fox said from the fireside:

"When I clump, ta-ra!

When I thump, ta-ra!

When I jump, ta-ra-ra!

How the fur flies!"

And at that, the bull was frightened, and he ran away.
And the hare walked on.

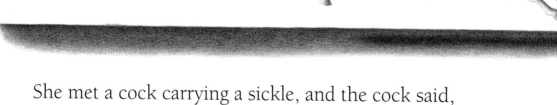

She met a cock carrying a sickle, and the cock said,
"What are you crying for?"

"I can't help it," said the hare. "I made a hut of tree bark, and the
fox made a hut of ice. He begged me to let him in, and now he
drives me out."

"Don't cry," said the cock. "I'll get rid of him."

"No, you won't," said the hare.

"The dog tried . . .

and the bear tried . . .

and the bull tried . . .
and they couldn't."

"Yes, I shall," said the cock. And he went to the hut, and said:

"Cock-a-doodle-do!   Cock-a-doodle-do!

I've a sickle on my shoulder!

I shall cut the fox in two!

Cock-a-doodle-do!"

And now it was the fox who was frightened.
"I'm getting dressed!" he said.

And the cock said:

"Cock-a-doodle-do! Cock-a-doodle-do!
I've a sickle on my shoulder!
I shall cut the fox in two!
Cock-a-doodle-do!"

The fox said, "I'm putting my fur on!"
But the cock said:

"Cock-a-doodle-do! Cock-a-doodle-do!
I've a sickle on my shoulder!
I shall cut the fox in two!
Cock-a-doodle-do!"

Out ran the fox! And after him,
slish-slash, went the cock with his
sickle, up the road! And when the
cock came back, he stayed with
the hare in the hut of tree bark.
And there they lived happy for
many a long day.

THE GIRL
AND THE GEESE

nce, an old man and his wife had a daughter and a son. And the mother said to the daughter, "Your father and I are off to market. While we are away, be very careful. Look after your little brother and don't, whatever you do, go out of the house."

"Yes, Mother," said the girl. But as soon as the old man and his wife were gone to market, she forgot what she had been told, and she left her brother sitting on the doorstep while she went out to play hopscotch in the street.

And while she was playing hopscotch, a flock of wild geese came down out of the sky, and lifted the little boy onto their wings and flew away with him.

The girl saw the geese, and she ran after them, but they flew into a dark wood.

The girl ran to the wood, and she saw a stove. And she said:

> "Stove, stove!
> Tell! Tell!
> Where have the geese gone?"

And the stove said, "Eat the burnt cake that is in my oven, and I shall tell you where the geese have gone."

> *But the girl wouldn't,*
> *so the stove didn't,*
> *and the girl ran on.*

She came to an apple tree, and she said:

> "Tree, tree!
> Tell! Tell!
> Where have the geese gone?"

And the tree said, "Eat the sharp apple that is on my branch, and I shall tell you where the geese have gone."

But the girl wouldn't,
so the tree didn't,
and the girl ran on.

She came to a brook of milk with banks of pies, and she said:

"Brook, brook!
Tell! Tell!
Where have the geese gone?"

And the brook said, "Drink my sour milk and eat my sad pies, and I shall tell you where the geese have gone."

But the girl wouldn't,
so the brook didn't,
and the girl ran on.

She met a pig in the wood, and she said:

"Pig, pig!
　　Tell! Tell!
　　　　Where have the geese gone?"

"Into my sty," said the pig, "and thrown me out, they have! That's where the geese have gone!"

The girl ran till she came to the sty in the middle of the wood. And there was her little brother, sitting on the floor in the mire, and he was playing with apples of gold and apples of silver.

The girl crept into the sty, picked up her brother in her arms, and ran out again.

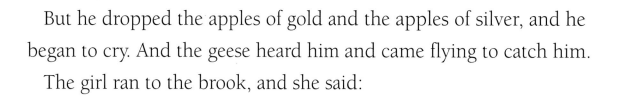

But he dropped the apples of gold and the apples of silver, and he began to cry. And the geese heard him and came flying to catch him.

The girl ran to the brook, and she said:

"Brook! Brook!
　　Hide me!
　　　　So the wild geese won't find me!"

And the brook said, "Drink my sour milk, and eat my sad pies."

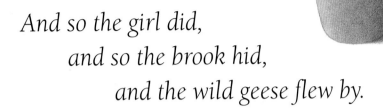

And so the girl did,
and so the brook hid,
and the wild geese flew by.

The girl ran on, and soon she heard the geese coming after, and she ran to the apple tree, and she said:

"Tree! Tree!
Hide me!
So the wild geese won't find me!"

And the tree said, "Eat my sharp apple."

And so the girl did,
and so the tree hid,
and the wild geese flew by.

The girl ran on, and soon she heard the geese coming after. And she came to the stove, and she said:

"Stove! Stove!
Hide me!
So the wild geese won't find me!"

And the stove said, "Eat my burnt cake."

*And so the girl did,
and so the stove hid,
and the wild geese flew by.*

The girl ran on. She ran out of the wood, and all the way home. And a good thing, too! For here come the old man and his wife, riding back from market!

BATTIBETH

Once upon a time and a long time, when bread was baked in ice and night began in the morning, there was a girl called Battibeth. Her mother was cooking the dinner, and she couldn't find her carving knife anywhere, so she sent Battibeth to borrow a knife from her grandmother. And with her she sent an egg, to give to her grandmother, for her kindness.

Battibeth ran to her grandmother's house. But on the way, she tripped and she fell, and the egg rolled out of her hand and she lost it. She picked herself up, and she saw that she had tripped over a penny so she took the penny to a shop, and she bought a needle. She took the needle to a blacksmith, and the blacksmith hammered the needle for her into a steeple.

Battibeth climbed the steeple. And from the top of the steeple she could see all the land around, and she saw that the egg had hatched into a cockerel and was threshing corn for a farmer in his barn.

She went to the farmer, and "Give me back my cockerel," she said. "And I want half the corn he has threshed, for his wages." So the farmer gave Battibeth the corn, and she loaded it onto the cockerel's back and set off for home.

Now the farmer had cheated Battibeth, and he had mixed corn and acorns together. And when Battibeth sat down to rest, the acorns sprouted and grew, so that when she got up, there were oak trees standing on the cockerel's back, and crows nesting in the oak trees, and boys were throwing clods of earth to scare the crows away.

They threw so many clods that when Battibeth climbed the oak trees she found enough soil up there to make a field; so she dug the field and planted turnips.

And when the turnips were grown, Battibeth picked one and broke it open.

In the turnip she saw a town. And by now Battibeth was hungry, so she went into the town to get a bowl of soup. The soup was so good that she drank it all up and licked the bowl clean.

There was a hair at the bottom of the bowl, and it stuck to Battibeth's tongue. She pulled the hair off her tongue, but the hair was fastened to leather reins, and at the end of the reins was a team of plow horses. The horses came out of the bowl one by one; and tied to the tail of the last horse was her mother's carving knife.

"And that," said Battibeth, "is the end of the tail."

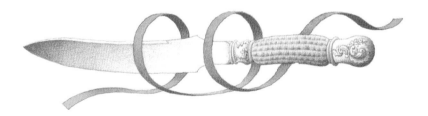

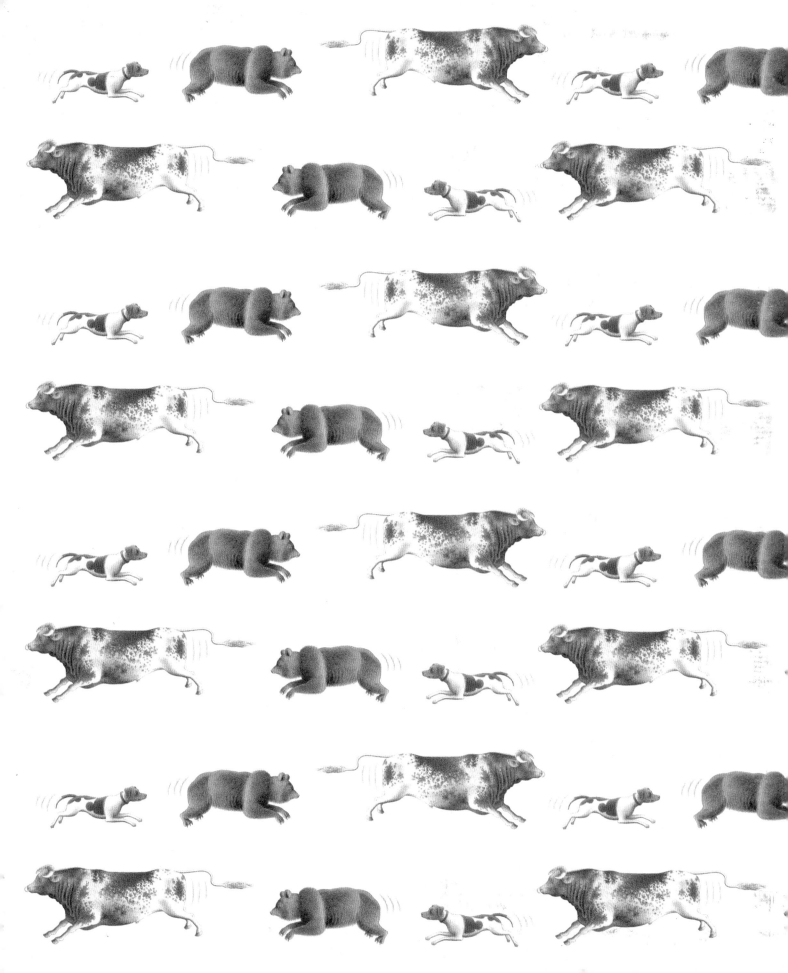